The King's Crown

Written by Suzie Good

Illustrated by Steve Bayley

British Library Cataloguing in Publication Data. A catalogue record for this book is available from the British Library.

Published in the United Kingdom by Onion Custard Kids, an imprint of Wordcatcher Publishing Group Ltd

First Edition: 2019 | Print edition ISBN: 9781789422771 | Ebook edition ISBN: 9781789422788

One morning in Buckingham Palace,

as the Queen was sipping her tea,

she said, "I'm retiring from ruling.

It's time I did something for me."

"Bucket lists seem to be trendy,

so I've written one for an ex-Queen.

Next Tuesday I start number one:

zip-wiring across a ravine."

Prince Chuck nearly choked on his muesli!

Did that mean he would be King?

She added, "You need to get ready.

On Monday your reign will begin."

Queen Betty then passed her old crown

to the butler, Benjamin Berkley.

She whispered, "It looks a bit grubby,

please clean it and make it look sparkly."

Berkley took the crown to the laundry

and saw it was covered in smears.

He wasn't surprised it was dirty –

she'd worn it for sixty-odd years!

After cleaning the diamonds and rubies,

then mending its delicate trim,

the crown shone bright like a glitterball.

A crown that was fit for the King.

Holding the historical headpiece,

and while there was no-one else there,

Berkley placed the crown on his head

pretending to be the Queen's heir.

He thought being King would be groovy.

He thought being King would be cool.

With two birthdays, a palace, three castles

and millions of people to rule.

Lost in his sovereign-daydream,

when a jingling bell cut it short.

The Prince was ringing for jodhpurs

for polo, his favourite sport.

So, Berkley tried to remove it,

but the crown was stuck on his head.

He pulled it left and pushed it right,

but it just got tighter instead.

He wiggled it and waggled it.

He gave it a twist and a turn.

He jiggled it and jangled it,

but it was stuck fast and firm.

DING-A-LING! The bell rang again.

The Prince was getting impatient.

If Berkley couldn't move the crown,

they'd need a butler replacement!

For help, he ran to the kitchen.

He found the head chef, Monsieur Chip.

When he saw what Berkley was wearing

he choked on his red-pepper dip.

"Ooh la la!" said Queen Betty's chef.

"You must make it slippy with grease."

So they poured olive oil on his head,

but the crown still wouldn't release.

They tried more slimy condiments:

ketchup, mayonnaise, even jelly.

But the crown wouldn't budge at all –

just made Berkley's hair a bit smelly.

Then he tried Her Majesty's salon,

where the Queen has her shampoo and set.

"Darling," said the stylist, "No problem.

Of course it will move when it's wet."

Leaning back with his head in the sink,

Berkley's hair and the crown had a wash.

But soap and bubbles wouldn't budge it –

though his hair now looked very posh!

Next, Berkley tried Buckingham Garage,

where they kept the Queen's favourite car.

They tried windscreen wash and some oil,

a wrench and a massive crowbar.

After all the twisting and pulling,

poor Berkley's head started to hurt.

The white woolly trim then got ripped

and a diamond fell off in the dirt!

"WITH A LEFT AND A RIGHT – ATTENSHUN!"

Outside they were changing the Guard.

Berkley asked the Captain for help.

"YES, SIR! It can't be that hard."

So, five Royal Guards pulled the crown
and four (plus a horse) pulled his feet.
But the stubborn crown was stuck tight,
as if it was fixed with concrete.

Feeling sore and quite over-stretched,

Berkley knew he had to confess.

Returning, he went past the nursery

full of children in fancy dress.

Inspired by their snazzy outfits,

and with help from his new-found friends,

Berkley asked to borrow some paper,

plus feathers, foil and felt pens.

They scissored, stuck and they sprinkled.

All happy to help and take part.

They pinned, papier mâchéd and painted,

to make a royal work of art.

"But what can I do to hide this?"

moaned Berkley about the old crown.

The kids found a big bowler hat –

the size of a sink and dark brown.

"At last – I've been ringing for ages,"

said Prince Chuck in a bit of a huff.

"I'm awfully sorry, Your Majesty,

I was giving your crown a quick buff."

Berkley passed the crown to the Prince,

who smiled and approved of the bling.

He liked it bigger and brighter,

so much more fitting for a King.

The Coronation Day was just splendid.

The new crown made everyone clap,

oblivious that the King's Butler

hid the real one under his hat.